Understanding the Elements of the Periodic Table™

POTASSIUM

Greg Roza

19 **39**

K

rosen publishing's
**rosen
central**®

New York

For Daisy

Published in 2008 by The Rosen Publishing Group, Inc.
29 East 21st Street, New York, NY 10010

First Edition

Library of Congress Cataloging-in-Publication Data

Roza, Greg.
Potassium / Greg Roza.
    p. cm. — (Understanding the elements of the periodic table)
Includes bibliographical references and index.
ISBN-13: 978-1-4042-1964-9
ISBN-10: 1-4042-1964-1
1. Potassium—Juvenile literature. 2. Periodic law—Tables—Juvenile literature. I. Title.
QD181.K1R69 2007
546'.383—dc22

                                                          2006101415

Manufactured in China

On the cover: Potassium's square on the periodic table of elements. Inset: Model of potassium's subatomic structure.

Contents

Introduction 4

Chapter One   The History of Potassium   6

Chapter Two   Potassium and the
Periodic Table   12

Chapter Three   Finding Potassium   23

Chapter Four   The Many Uses of
Potassium Compounds   28

Chapter Five   Potassium and You   35

The Periodic Table of Elements   40

Glossary   42

For More Information   43

For Further Reading   45

Bibliography   45

Index   47

What do you think of when you hear the word "potassium"? You may know that potassium can be found in the earth and the oceans or that the banana you had for lunch is loaded with it. However, did you know that potassium also exists as a metal that can be cut with a knife? Were you aware that it is an element found in many common salts? Have you heard that potassium metal reacts violently when combined with water? Potassium is an element that may surprise you. It takes many forms and is used for many surprising purposes.

Many centuries ago, people began using plant ashes to make their lives easier, such as by using them as a form of soap. A long time later, scientists discovered that plant ashes contain a substantial amount of the element potassium. Our understanding of potassium has come a long way. Today, potassium and potassium compounds are used for many purposes, some of which may surprise you.

Consider the case of potassium superoxide. This compound is made by burning pure liquid potassium in a chamber filled with pure oxygen gas. The superoxide compound that results is used in a modern invention called a rebreather. Rebreathers are similar to scuba tanks used by deep-sea divers. Instead of compressed oxygen, however, rebreathers carry potassium superoxide. Rebreathers work by combining potassium superoxide with carbon dioxide, which comes from the lungs when a diver exhales. A chemical reaction takes place between the two compounds. They join to make two new substances—potassium carbonate and oxygen. The oxygen can be breathed safely. Rebreathers are smaller and lighter than traditional air tanks, and they allow divers to stay underwater longer.

Underwater isn't the only place where potassium superoxide comes in handy. The Russian Space Agency, for example, uses potassium superoxide as a chemical oxygen generator on spacecrafts and for space suits. Firefighters also use similar oxygen-generating gear when battling intense blazes that involve smoke. Rebreathers keep firefighters safe in hostile environments. Potassium superoxide is just one of the many valuable and often surprising uses of potassium.

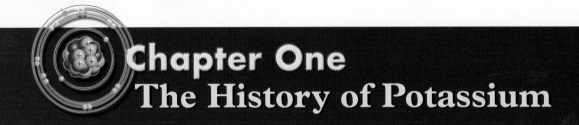

Chapter One
The History of Potassium

Potassium is the seventh-most abundant element on Earth. It is essential for nearly all life. Potassium compounds are used for many reasons—from seasoning food to dating very old rocks. However, many people know very little about it. There are several reasons for this.

Despite the fact that potassium is found in dozens of natural compounds and hundreds of industrial products, it rarely exists in its pure form as a metal. Pure potassium metal reacts quickly with oxygen and moisture in the air, which is a process called corrosion. Potassium metal must be stored in a liquid such as mineral oil to minimize the oxygen and water exposure to the metal to prevent corrosion. Due to the fact that potassium metal reacts so quickly with other elements, it is not found naturally as a metal but in compounds with other elements. Thus, scientists did not know that it was an element until 1807.

Potash

Potassium is very important to living things. Plants need potassium to grow tall and strong—their cells contain significant amounts of the element. A long time ago, people all over the world discovered that the ashes left over after burning plants could be used to flavor foods. Although these

Here, a young boy is slashing and burning fields, readying the soil for growing crops with the aid of potash.

ashes contain many impurities, wood and plant ashes also contain a potassium salt called potassium carbonate (K_2CO_3). Native Americans and people in Asia also used wood ash to preserve meats.

At some point, someone decided to soak plant ashes in water and boil them in a pot. The result was a more pure form of potassium carbonate that could be used to make soap and glass. The English named this substance potash because it was prepared by boiling ashes in a pot. In the seventeenth century, people began to notice that spreading potash in their gardens helped their plants grow. Another potassium compound that people commonly used was potassium hydroxide, or caustic potash. This is a substance similar to lye (sodium hydroxide, $NaOH$), and it is sometimes called potash lye. This was made by baking potash in a kiln to remove even more impurities along with carbon dioxide (CO_2). The result was a fine white powder.

Potash and other potassium salts—such as potassium chloride, also called sylvite—were eventually found in and around ancient sea beds. Potassium-rich minerals were also discovered in Earth's crust. In 1797, a German scientist named Martin Klaproth found potash in a volcanic rock in Italy. Scientists eventually found potassium in other rocks, particularly in feldspar, a component of granite. As more potassium compounds were discovered, "potash" became a catchall term for most potassium compounds, which sometimes resulted in confusion.

For many years, scientists thought that potash was an elemental substance (meaning that it could not be broken down any further). It was also confused with a similar substance commonly called soda ash, or sodium carbonate. However, one scientist questioned these assertions

and worked to prove them wrong. Sir Humphry Davy first isolated potassium from caustic potash in 1807. Davy used a process called electrolysis, which involved passing an electric current through a sample, in this case through molten caustic potash. It was the first metal to be isolated in this manner. Others quickly followed.

Shown here is a portrait of Martin Klaproth. Klaproth was the most important chemist of his time in Germany.

Davy immediately named this substance potassium, a term he derived from the word "potash."

Potassium and potassium compounds have been used for numerous applications. Today, potassium chloride is one of the most common industrial chemicals. About 95 percent of the potassium refined today is used in the manufacture of fertilizers. Aside from fertilizer, soap, and glass, potassium compounds have also been used to manufacture explosives, gunpowder, medicines, and many other products. The methods for obtaining and refining potassium have also improved over the years.

Sir Humphry Davy

Sir Humphry Davy (1778–1829) was the English chemist who discovered potassium, but he is known for other important chemistry milestones. Thanks to the discoveries of Italian scientist Alessandro Volta—who developed the first working battery—Davy began experimenting with the electrolysis of salts using batteries. Davy was convinced that some substances that were considered elemental, such as potash, could actually be broken down into smaller parts. After several trials, Davy successfully isolated potassium by running an electrical current through an iron plate that held molten caustic potash. Davy was elated to see small globs of a silvery metal forming from the caustic potash. He named the metal globs potassium.

Over the next few years, Davy went on to isolate other metals using similar techniques, including sodium (Na), calcium (Ca), strontium (Sr), barium (Ba), and magnesium (Mg). Davy was knighted for his discoveries in 1812. French ruler Napoléon Bonaparte awarded him a medal in 1813.

This is a 1931 version of the electrolysis equipment Sir Humphry Davy used to isolate potassium. Modern electrolysis equipment hasn't changed much since Davy's day.

The Periodic Table

The periodic table is a useful chart of the elements. The table allows scientists to conveniently see the relationships between elements. It can also be used to predict the occurrence and behavior of compounds combining the elements. Most periodic tables list basic attributes for each element.

In the years leading up to 1869, several chemists from around the world were close to organizing the known elements into a unified table. Scientists began to assemble elements into groups based on similarities they noticed between them. In 1869, a Russian chemist named Dmitry Mendeleyev developed an early form of the periodic table that we are familiar with today. Mendeleyev was not the first to derive such a table, but he was the best publicist for his system of the elements, so he is usually given the most credit. Mendeleyev assembled the elements based on their atomic weights. Once he did this, he realized that certain characteristics occurred in regular intervals, or periods.

Mendeleyev—and other chemists who followed his lead—left gaps in the table where he predicted new elements would appear once they were discovered. The predictions that Mendeleyev and others made were sometimes correct, which convinced skeptics of the value of this organizational tool. Over the years, other scientists refined and added to the periodic table. However, it still follows Mendeleyev's original concept.

Chapter Two
Potassium and the Periodic Table

Atoms are the basic building blocks of nature, and all matter in the universe is made up of them. The different types of atoms are known as chemical elements. To date, there are 116 known elements, but many scientists are still searching for and making new ones.

Atoms are unbelievably small. Even the smallest speck of matter that can be seen under a microscope contains billions of atoms. Each atom is made up of even smaller parts called subatomic particles.

Subatomic Particles

Subatomic particles are the tiny pieces that come together to make up a single atom. There are three kinds of subatomic particles that determine the chemical properties of an atom: protons, neutrons, and electrons. Protons have a positive electrical charge. Electrons have a negative electrical charge. Neutrons have no electrical charge. Protons and neutrons bunch together to make up the core of an atom. This core is called a nucleus. The nucleus is a very tiny part of an atom, but it makes up most of an atom's mass.

The area around the nucleus is mostly empty space and is where the electrons are found. Electrons have very little mass. They surround the nucleus in layers that are called shells. An atom can normally have up to seven

This is a diagram of a potassium atom. Notice that potassium has a single electron in its outer shell.

shells containing electrons. There can be a single electron in a shell, or there can be dozens. The exact number depends on the shell and the identity of the element. The first shell—the shell closest to the nucleus—never has more than two electrons. Atoms of potassium have two electrons in their first shell, eight in the second shell, eight in the third shell, and one electron in the fourth and outer shell. Elements like potassium that have a single electron in their outer shell can easily lose an electron. This makes these elements react very easily with other elements and compounds that can gain one or more electrons.

Categorizing Chemical Elements

Chemical elements are categorized in several ways. Each element has an atomic number, which is the number of protons in the atom. All atoms of an element have the same atomic number. All the elements of the periodic table are arranged in order based on their atomic numbers, from hydrogen (atomic number 1) to ununhexium (atomic number 116). The atomic number for potassium is 19, which means that an atom of potassium has 19 protons.

Potassium Snapshot

Chemical Symbol:	K
Classification:	Alkali metal
Properties:	Silvery-white and soft, exists as a solid at room temperature
Discovered by:	Sir Humphrey Davy in 1807
Atomic Number:	19
Atomic Weight:	39.10
Protons:	19
Electrons:	19 in the metallic form; 18 in the ionic form
Neutrons:	20
Density at 68° Fahrenheit (20° Celsius):	0.86 g/cm^3
Melting Point:	146°F (63°C)
Boiling Point:	1,398 °F (759 °C)
Commonly Found:	In the earth and the oceans

Atoms can also be categorized using their atomic weights. Atomic weight, also called atomic mass, is the mass of an atom. The atomic weight is the sum of the masses of all the electrons, protons, and neutrons in that atom. However, since the mass of an electron is tiny, the atomic mass for an atom can be closely approximated by totaling just the masses of its neutrons and protons. The periodic table lists potassium's average atomic weight as 39.10.

To understand why potassium's atomic weight is a fraction instead of the whole number 39, which is how it is often represented on the periodic

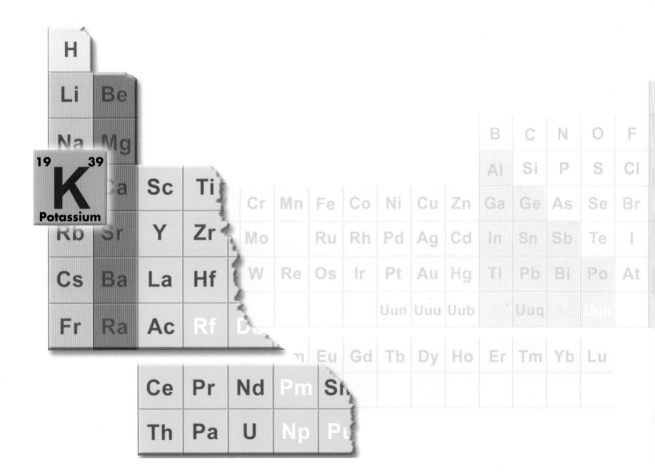

The periodic table is a convenient way to study and remember the elements. Potassium and the other alkali metals are in yellow.

table, it's important to understand that some atoms, such as potassium, have varying numbers of protons. These atoms are called isotopes, and they are all the same element with essentially the same properties, except for their different atomic masses. Potassium has three naturally occurring isotopes and more than a dozen additional isotopes that don't occur naturally. All these isotopes are still potassium, and they still occupy the same space on the periodic table. When we average the atomic weights of all the naturally occurring isotopes weighted by the percentage that each occurs, we get the atomic mass shown on the periodic table, of about 39.10.

Atoms of a particular element can also have a different number of electrons. An atom that has lost or gained an electron from the pure element that has the same number of electrons as protons is called an ion. Ions have a positive charge when they lose electrons because they end up with more protons (positive charges) in the atoms than electrons (negative charges), and a negative charge when they gain electrons because of an excess of negative charges in each atom. Potassium normally forms only ions with a +1 charge; it is these ions that are found naturally and play an important role in keeping animals cells alive. They are needed to keep our hearts beating and blood flowing through our bodies.

Groups and Periods

The periodic table organizes elements into sets called families or groups with similar chemical properties that result from having the same number of outer shell electrons. Groups form columns on the periodic table. Potassium is in group 1 of the periodic table, which is commonly called the alkali metals. All alkali metals have certain characteristics in common: they are soft, silvery metals that have one electron in their outermost shell, and they react easily to lose this electron to form compounds containing a potassium ion.

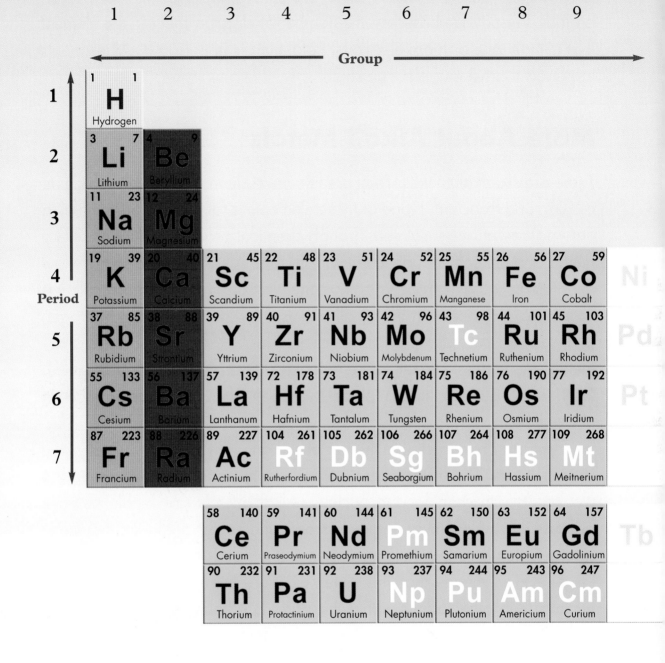

| | IA | IIA | IIIB | IVB | VB | VIB | VIIB | VIIIB | VIIIB |
| | 1 | 2 | 3 | 4 | 5 | 6 | 7 | 8 | 9 |

This periodic table shows the periods *(along the left side)* and the groups *(along the top)*. As you can see, potassium is in group 1, period 4.

The rows on the periodic table are called periods. There are seven periods. Periods are based on the number of electron shells in the element that contain one or more electrons. Potassium is in period 4. All elements in period 4 have four electron shells.

More About Alkali Metals

There are six alkali metals. They are lithium, sodium, potassium, rubidium, cesium, and francium. None of these elements is found as a pure metal in nature. They must be isolated through chemical processes. All are silvery metals and are soft enough to cut with a knife. Alkali metals also have low densities. Because hydrogen also has one electron in its outermost shell, it is sometimes grouped with the alkali metals. However, elemental hydrogen is a gas and can also gain an electron. This is different than the alkali metals and is more similar to the halogen group (fluorine [F] and down). Thus, some periodic tables place hydrogen above fluorine instead of above lithium.

Electrons are attracted to the nucleus of an atom, and they usually stay in their orbits. The farther an electron is from the nucleus, however, the weaker its attraction for the nucleus. Alkali metals are highly reactive because they have only a single electron in their outer shell, plus they have a larger atomic radius than other elements of the same period (row). The larger radius means that this outer electron is farther away from the nucleus than other atoms within the period. Alkali metal atoms have a single electron in their outer shells. This electron is lost easily to other elements and molecules that can accept that electron to form salts. These salts contain +1 potassium ions (cations, resulting from the loss of the single outer electron) along with negatively charged atoms or group of atoms (anions) to balance the charge. Alkali metals oxidize, or tarnish, rapidly in air by their reaction with oxygen in the air. They react easily

The alkali metals lithium, sodium, and potassium are stored in oil to keep them from reacting with the air. The photo to the right shows potassium reacting with water.

with the group of elements called halogens (which includes fluorine and chlorine) to create salts containing potassium cations and halogen anions. They also react readily with water, which can generate enough heat energy to ignite the hydrogen that is created during the reaction. For this reason, alkali metals are often stored in mineral oil. Although other alkalis are even more reactive, potassium is the most reactive common metal on the periodic table.

Reactivity Series of Common Metals

A reactivity or activity series of metals is an arrangement of metals listed in order of reactivity. Scientists and students can use a reactivity series to help predict what will happen during an experiment involving the elements that appear on it. A reactivity series can also be used to show how a metal will react with other substances, such as water and acids. A metal can replace metals lower than it on the list, but not metals higher than it. Potassium often appears at the very top of reactivity series, since it is the most reactive common metal.

Acids and Bases

Acids are compounds that form positively charged hydrogen ions when dissolved in water. A hydrogen ion is an atom of hydrogen that has lost its only electron, leaving a single proton, which bears a positive charge. The more hydrogen ions an acid forms in water for the same amount of starting acid, the stronger the acid is. Strong acids in sufficient quantities can eat through clothes, skin, and even some harder materials.

Bases are compounds that form negatively charged hydroxide ions when dissolved in water. Hydroxide ions are made up of an atom of oxygen and an atom of hydrogen, plus one extra electron to give a negative charge. Bases, such as some potassium compounds like potassium hydroxide (KOH), are also called alkalis. Depending on how strong and concentrated they are, bases can also be quite dangerous. On the other hand, some are perfectly safe household items when used properly. Bases often form slippery-feeling solutions when combined with water, and many are used to make soaps and detergents.

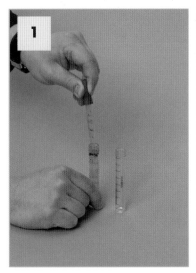

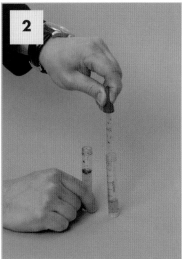

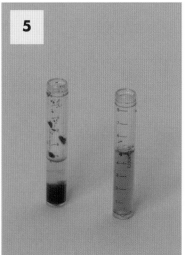

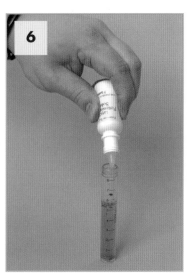

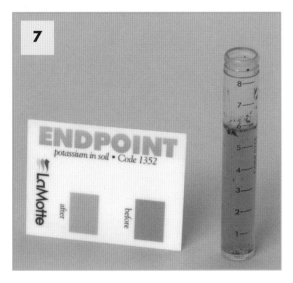

This experiment shows the amount of potassium in soil. Transfer the potassium extracting solution mixed with soil to a clean test tube (1, 2). Add a potassium indicator tablet (3). Cap and mix the tube until the tablet dissolves (4, 5). Add potassium test solution in two-drop intervals (6). Stop when the solution turns blue (7).

The pH scale is a measurement of the concentration (amount per unit volume) of hydrogen ions in a solution ("pH" stands for "potential hydrogen"). The lower the pH number, the more acidic the solution. The higher the number, the more alkaline or basic the solution. Strong acids and bases react to neutralize each other if combined in equal quantities. This means that they combine to form compounds that are neither acidic nor alkaline, often water and a salt.

Some potassium compounds are bases, not because of the potassium cation in those compounds but because of the anions that are needed to give a neutral compound. For example, potassium hydroxide (made up of the ions K+ and OH–) is highly caustic (it can cause burns and holes in clothing for instance) and should be handled only by a trained chemist. Most strongly alkaline potassium compounds are used in fertilizers and chemical cleansers. Others can be used safely in the home if the directions given with the product are followed closely. You may even find some potassium compounds—such as cream of tartar (a weak base)—in your kitchen cabinets.

Chapter Three
Finding Potassium

Potassium-containing compounds are often lumped under the common term "potash." Chemically speaking, however, not all potassium compounds are potash. For many years, scientists believed that potash was an "elemental" substance—that it could not be broken down into other substances. Up until the eighteenth century, there was also no distinction made between potassium and sodium. This is partially because their compounds look similar and because they are often found in the same locations. Thanks to Sir Humphry Davy, other scientists began identifying potassium in substances they had known about for years. The more scientists learned about potassium, the more natural compounds they were able to identify that contain potassium ions.

Potassium Sources

Potassium can be obtained from the earth, seawater, plants, and animal droppings. Potassium is the seventh-most abundant element on the earth. It is the eighth-most abundant element in the earth's crust, making up about 2 percent of its weight. It is most often found in minerals such as feldspar, sylvite (KCl), and micas. It is the fifth-most abundant element in seawater. Seawater contains approximately 0.75 grams of potassium per liter (a liter is a little more than one quart), about thirty times less than sodium. The lower

This is perthite, a variety of feldspar. The blue layers, called microcline, contain potassium. Microcline is used in the manufacture of porcelain and glass.

potassium concentration in seawater is the result of potassium ion being held more tightly in the soils and because most potassium ions that dissolve into surface waters are scavenged by plants (in fact, the growth of wild plants is frequently limited by the potassium supply), so less potassium ions proceed to the oceans in those surface waters. However, potassium is never found free in its metallic form in nature; it is always found as the ion.

The first source of potassium for fertilizer and soap came from plant ashes. Another early source was niter deposits. Niter is a white crystal that forms over many years when water seeps through limestone deposits in caves. Once plentiful, this source has nearly disappeared. However, niter is simply the natural form of potassium nitrate. Today, potassium nitrate is made by mixing sodium nitrate with a solution of potassium chloride. The potassium nitrate is the least soluble component of the resulting mixture, so the solids containing this compound can be separated from the solution containing sodium chloride.

Scientists began identifying potassium compounds in the earth's crust and in the oceans in the 1800s. They realized that there was a seemingly limitless supply of the valuable element to be harvested. Many deposits in the Earth's crust were formed from ancient plant life. As these plants died, the potassium contained in them turned to potash and other potassium compounds over the course of many centuries.

Refining Potassium

Originally, potash was created by burning plants. Over the years, the process was improved upon. Impurities were first removed from the ashes formed by burning plants by running water through these ashes. This water was then boiled, leaving a purer form of potash. Pure potassium carbonate was first made by baking potash in a kiln. The result was a fine white powder that was sometimes called pearlash (essentially purified potash). Historically, pearlash has been used for a number of purposes,

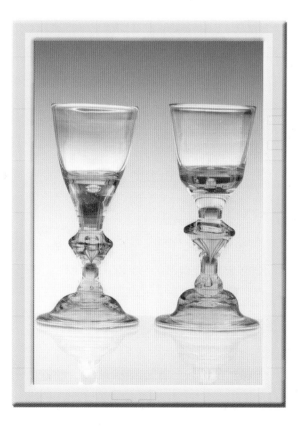

These goblets are made of potash glass, from which many glass products were made. They were manufactured in the mid-eighteenth century.

Twentieth-Century Potassium Shortage

At one time, the largest known source of potassium minerals in the world was in Stassfurt, Germany. Farmers in the United States once bought the sylvite that was mined in Germany to put on their crops. A by-product of the mining operations and a compound that can be made from other potassium compounds such as potash is saltpeter (potassium nitrate, KNO_3), an important ingredient in gunpowder. During World War II, Adolf Hitler and the Nazis stopped shipping sylvite to the Allied countries. This initially resulted in a potassium shortage. The Allied countries needed potash to make gunpowder. The United States needed to devise a way to obtain its own potassium. Scientists searched for potassium sources in the United States and found two large deposits in Searles Lake, California, and Carlsbad, New Mexico. This led to the development of modern brine-harvesting techniques.

Scientists had been searching for other alternatives since the early 1900s. Perhaps the most interesting alternative came from a potassium-rich aquatic plant. In 1916, the United States opened kelp-refining factories on the coast of California. The kelp was grown, harvested, and burned to increase the supplies of potash.

including the manufacture of soap, glass, and china. It was even used as a leavening agent before the discovery of baking powder.

Pure Potassium

As mentioned in chapter 2, alkali metals have a high level of reactivity; potassium is the most reactive of the common metals. For this reason,

Shown here is a chunk of pure potassium metal. It is shiny because it was freshly cut just before the photo was taken.

potassium is never found free in nature as the metal. Pure potassium metal reacts so quickly with many other elements and compounds—particularly oxygen and water in the air—that it must be stored under a layer of mineral oil. The mineral oil keeps the potassium from reacting with oxygen, which makes up about 20 percent of air, as well as with moisture in the air.

Since it so difficult to keep potassium in its pure or metallic form, potassium metal actually has relatively few uses. Potassium compounds, however, have been used for centuries for many reasons—from baking bread to waging wars.

Chapter Four
The Many Uses of Potassium Compounds

Although pure potassium metal has only a few specialized applications, potassium compounds are quite common and are extremely useful for a variety of purposes. Potash and other potassium compounds have been used for centuries in the manufacture of glass products. Potassium aluminum silicate, commonly called orthoclase, is mined for its aluminum content, but it is also used to make glass, ceramics, and porcelain. The potassium in orthoclase makes glass stronger and scratch resistant. Other common industrial uses for potassium compounds include desiccants (drying agents), cotton dyes, disinfectants, baking supplies, food additives/preservatives, and batteries.

Fertilizers

Plants require a number of essential nutrients to grow and be healthy. Potassium ions are one of these nutrients. Plants get potassium ions and other nutrients from the soil in which they grow. When plants die, they rot and turn back into soil. This returns valuable nutrients to the earth for new plants to use. On farms and in many gardens, however, some or all of the plants are taken out of the soil in which they grow. This removes some of the nutrients. After a while, that soil may not have enough nutrients to sustain healthy plant life. Potassium ions and other

Bags of fertilizer are stacked in neat rows outside of the factory in which they were manufactured in Ince, England.

nutrients must be put back into the soil in the form of fertilizers to renew that soil.

Today, 95 percent of the potassium compounds gathered in the world is used in the manufacture of fertilizers. The potassium compound most

How Plants Use Potassium

Plants take potassium ions and other nutrients from the soil through their roots. Many of these nutrients enter the plant as ions. Plants use potassium ions (K+) to help build strong cell walls. This allows them to grow tall and strong. It also allows them to survive in relatively cold or hot weather.

Some plants use more potassium ions than others. Apple trees do not use a lot. Dandelions, on the other hand, require a lot of potassium ions to survive. For this reason, the fertilizer that people use on their lawns is often low in potassium sources. This helps to inhibit the growth of dandelions.

Dandelion leaves are so high in potassium that some people eat them to increase the potassium in their diets. Dandelion leaves are also high in vitamins A, B, C, and D.

commonly used in the manufacture of fertilizers today is potassium chloride. When combined with nitrogen and phosphorus compounds, potassium fertilizers are perfect for returning much-needed nutrients to the soil.

Soaps and Cleansers

Soaps are made from alkalis containing potassium and sodium ions plus a plant oil or animal fat. Most soaps used today are made from sodium

Potassium is prevalent in our everyday lives; most of the household products pictured here contain potassium compounds.

hydroxide. Potassium hydroxide and potassium carbonate are commonly used to make potassium-based soaps. Some soaps use a combination of these two alkalis. Potassium soaps are usually softer than sodium soaps. For this reason, shaving cream, hand lotions, and liquid hand soaps often contain weak potassium compounds. These include potassium sorbate and potassium stearate.

Many strong cleansers are made from or contain potassium hydroxide. Drain and oven cleaners often have potassium hydroxide in them. When a drain is clogged with grease, potassium hydroxide can react with the fat to effectively turn it into a soap. This soap dissolves in water and washes away. Potassium hydroxide is a strong alkali, or base, and can cause painful burns. This is because it breaks down the fat and oils in the top layers of skin, essentially turning them into a crude soap.

Boom!

When you hear the world "explosive," you probably think of bombs booming and bullets flying. However, there are many useful functions for explosive chemicals beyond military applications. An explosion is a chemical reaction that quickly releases a significant amount of heat, usually along with gaseous products. Many types of explosions—like those caused by some potassium compounds—involve a chemical known as an oxidizing agent.

An oxidizing agent, or oxidizer, facilitates the removal of electrons from another compound because the oxidizing agent is good at accepting electrons. Sometimes this process quickly releases a lot of heat, creating the potential for ignition, as well as gaseous products, which can create an explosion. Potassium permanganate, for example, is a common oxidizing agent.

Gunpowder and Fireworks

The first explosive was gunpowder. Gunpowder was invented by the Chinese about 2,000 years ago. This explosive chemical is made by combining potassium nitrate, sulfur, and carbon. When lit, gunpowder burns to forms potassium carbonate, potassium sulfate, carbon dioxide, nitrogen, and small amounts of other products. Gunpowder ignites to make a powerful blast because of the large amount of heat and gaseous products that are produced. Over the centuries, different ingredients and amounts were used in the manufacture of gunpowder to make it stronger

Potassium compounds are frequently used in fireworks because they release a large amount of oxygen, which allows them to burn more easily.

or weaker, depending on the purpose. Today, explosives are made from a variety of chemicals, but potassium compounds remain one of the most common.

If you've ever watched a fireworks display, you have seen great quantities of potassium compounds exploding high in the air. Most of these compounds are forms of gunpowder. In fact, fireworks were probably one of the earliest uses of the flammable powder. The different colors and shapes you see when fireworks explode are a result of the different chemicals used to make them and the ways that those chemicals are packed in the charge. For instance, sodium salts make a yellow color, and barium creates a green explosion.

Potassium-Argon Dating

Using a process called potassium-argon dating, geologists can tell approximately how old a rock actually is. Many rocks contain a potassium isotope known as potassium-40 (K-40). This isotope is radioactive. That means that it undergoes nuclear decay, which can change the number of protons in the nucleus to turn an atom into another element. K-40 atoms decay to form argon-40 (Ar-40) atoms over a long period of time. Argon-40 is a rare gas, and the decay rate to form Ar-40 from K-40 is known.

As the K-40 in rocks decays and forms Ar-40, the Ar-40 gas remains trapped in the rocks. By melting a rock to liberate the Ar-40 gas and measuring the ratio of K-40 to Ar-40 in it, geologists can determine about how old the rock is. The oldest rocks dated by the process were approximately 3.7 to 3.8 billion years old.

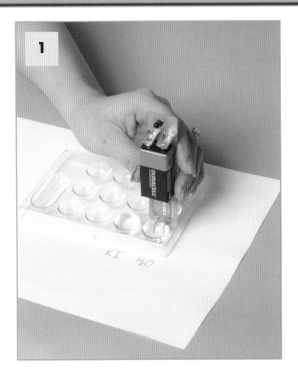
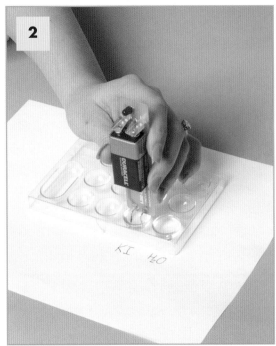

When an electric current is passed through distilled water, the lightbulb does not light up (1). When potassium chloride is added to the water, it conducts electricity and the bulb illuminates (2).

Potassium Compounds: The Downside

Although potassium compounds are highly useful, they can also be very dangerous. Potassium-based fireworks and explosives are unsafe to handle. Leave those compounds to the experts. Also, an extreme overdose of potassium-containing medicine can cause the heart to beat erratically. In extreme cases, this can lead to death.

The overuse of potassium-containing fertilizers can pollute nearby bodies of water. The resulting high mineral content of the water can cause an excessive increase in other organisms, such as algae. This overgrowth of algae can kill off marine animal and plant life by consuming their needed nutrients, such as oxygen.

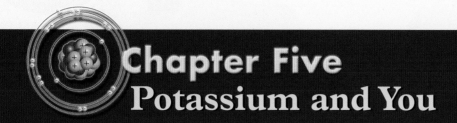

Chapter Five
Potassium and You

In the previous chapter, we learned that potassium ions are very important to plant growth. They are also very important to human health. Potassium ions are found in a majority of the foods we eat; after all, it is an important ion for both plants and animals. According to its Web site, the Institute of Medicine of the National Academies recommends that adults get 4,700 milligrams of potassium every day. Potassium ions are in so many foods that the average person usually gets as much as half of that amount every day without eating a lot of potassium-rich foods. Some foods, like bananas and spinach, have relatively high concentrations of potassium ions. If you need to boost your daily intake of potassium ions, fresh fruits and vegetables, meat, and milk are the best sources. Processed foods, such as frozen dinners, are usually very low in potassium ions and high in sodium ions.

The human body uses potassium ions for many important functions. Without potassium ions, we would simply not be able to remain alive. This is why it is so important that people get plenty of potassium every day.

Pumping Potassium

Electrolytes are important to the human body because they are able to balance charges as well as conduct electricity—which is essentially the

Bananas and spinach are two important sources of potassium. The average banana contains about 420 milligrams of potassium. One cup of raw spinach contains about 170 milligrams.

flow of electrons from one area to another. Potassium (and sodium) ions are vital to the proper functioning of the nervous system and the muscles.

Before a nerve impulse is sent through a cell in the nervous system, there are potassium ions inside the cell and sodium ions outside the cell. This is actually the opposite of how cells normally like things.

When an electrical impulse is sent through the nervous system, the potassium and sodium ions switch places. This allows the electrical impulse to travel where it needs to go. After this occurs, the cells need to "reset." Structures on the cell walls "pump" the potassium ions back in and the sodium ions out. Now the cell is once again prepared to transmit an electrical impulse. The NaK pump is also important to the proper functioning of the heart. Without it, our hearts could not beat and pump blood through our veins.

What Are Electrolytes?

Potassium ions and some other important nutrients occur in the human body as electrolytes. Electrolytes are ions. Ions, as we have already learned, are atoms or groups of atoms with an overall positive or negative charge. Atoms that lose an electron are positively charged because they have more protons than electrons. Atoms that gain an electron are negatively charged because they have more electrons than protons.

All potassium atoms in the human body are found as positive ions. Potassium ions are the most common electrolyte in the human body. An adult body that weighs 155 pounds contains approximately 4 ounces of potassium ions. Most potassium ions are located in the red blood cells, but many are also located in the cells of the nervous system and the muscles.

Potassium and Digestion

Potassium electrolytes play an important role in the digestion, or breaking down, of the food we eat. Without effective digestion, our bodies would not be able to get nutrients from food. It would also be impossible to pass waste products through out digestive systems.

When we chew food, our mouths add saliva, or spit, to the food. This saliva contains, among other components, sodium, potassium, and chloride electrolytes. These electrolytes help to soften the food so that it is easier to swallow.

Once food reaches the stomach, potassium ions really start to work. The stomach contains a fluid that aids in digesting food. A pump similar to the NaK pump, called the potassium-ion pump, removes potassium ions from the digestive fluid. The pump replaces potassium ions with hydrogen ions, which along with the chlorine ions creates hydrochloric acid (HCl).

Potassium and Blood Pressure

The amount of force that your beating heart exerts on your blood vessels is called blood pressure. This amount changes in different situations. Hypertension is the medical term for high blood pressure. The heart of a person with high blood pressure has to work extra hard to pump blood throughout the body. In some cases, this can lead to a loss of blood flow in the brain, which is called a stroke.

Scientists believe that hypertension can be caused by too many sodium ions in your diet or not enough potassium ions. This can be the result of not eating enough fresh fruit and vegetables or by eating too many processed foods and table salt. Studies show that people who get plenty of potassium ions in their daily diet are less likely to suffer from hypertension. They are also less likely to have strokes.

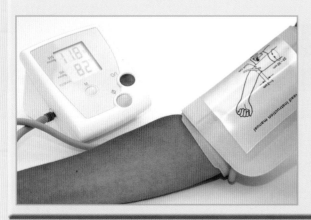

It is important to have your blood pressure checked on a regular basis. Some people take potassium supplements to help fight high blood pressure.

Hydrochloric acid, sometimes called stomach acid, is a strong acid. For example, hydrochloric acid is sometimes used to remove rust from steel. This powerful acid does not normally hurt the stomach because it is coated with a thick layer of mucus. Hydrochloric acid helps to break food down so it can be used by the body and so waste can be passed through the body. This process would not be possible without potassium ions.

Putting lots of green vegetables on your food is a good way of getting the potassium you need in your diet.

Heartburn

In some people, stomach acid can escape up out of the stomach into the esophagus. The acid burns the esophagus, creating a painful sensation called heartburn. In addition, excess hydrochloric acid can actually eat through the mucus in the stomach. This can eventually lead to painful and dangerous stomach sores called ulcers.

In chapter 2, we learned that acids and bases neutralize each other. People with heartburn and acid indigestion can take an antacid to relieve their pain. Antacids are medicines that contain a base. Potassium bicarbonate is a common antacid.

The potassium bicarbonate neutralizes some of the stomach acid. This usually causes the pain to go away.

Potassium in Your World

From plants to animals, from earth to seawater, and from our kitchen cabinets to our gardens, potassium ions are all around us. They are even inside of us! Potassium can do a lot, too. It can tell us the age of ancient rocks and help astronauts to breathe in outer space. Now that you know all about potassium, look for it in the products and objects in your every-day life. You might be surprised where you find it.

The Periodic Table of Elements

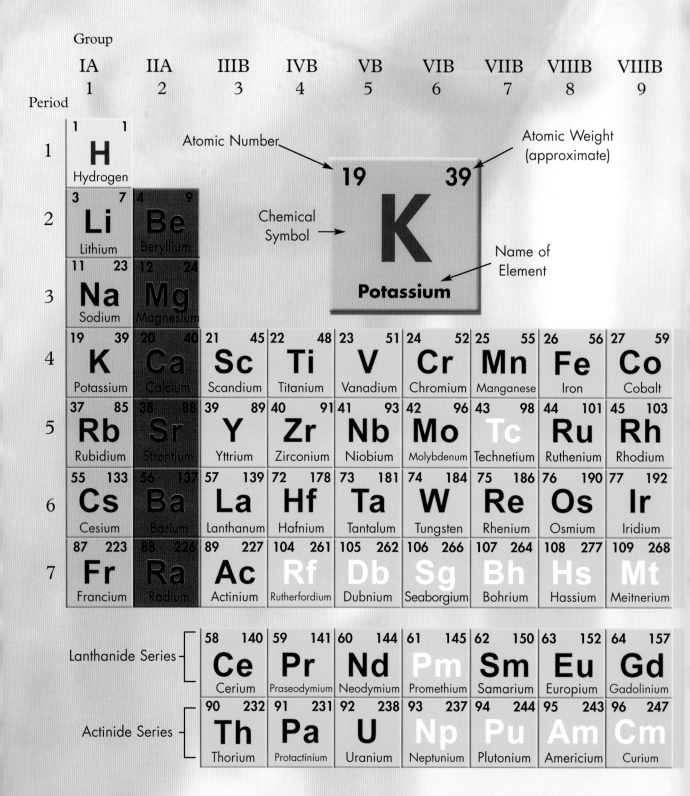

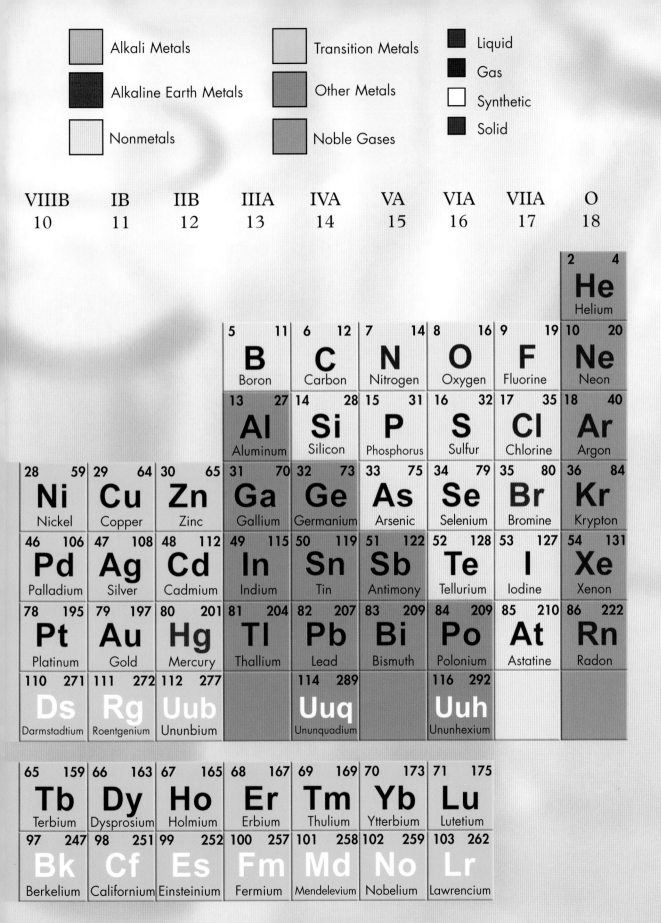

Legend

- Alkali Metals
- Alkaline Earth Metals
- Nonmetals
- Transition Metals
- Other Metals
- Noble Gases
- Liquid
- Gas
- Synthetic
- Solid

VIIIB 10	IB 11	IIB 12	IIIA 13	IVA 14	VA 15	VIA 16	VIIA 17	O 18
								2 4 **He** Helium
			5 11 **B** Boron	6 12 **C** Carbon	7 14 **N** Nitrogen	8 16 **O** Oxygen	9 19 **F** Fluorine	10 20 **Ne** Neon
			13 27 **Al** Aluminum	14 28 **Si** Silicon	15 31 **P** Phosphorus	16 32 **S** Sulfur	17 35 **Cl** Chlorine	18 40 **Ar** Argon
28 59 **Ni** Nickel	29 64 **Cu** Copper	30 65 **Zn** Zinc	31 70 **Ga** Gallium	32 73 **Ge** Germanium	33 75 **As** Arsenic	34 79 **Se** Selenium	35 80 **Br** Bromine	36 84 **Kr** Krypton
46 106 **Pd** Palladium	47 108 **Ag** Silver	48 112 **Cd** Cadmium	49 115 **In** Indium	50 119 **Sn** Tin	51 122 **Sb** Antimony	52 128 **Te** Tellurium	53 127 **I** Iodine	54 131 **Xe** Xenon
78 195 **Pt** Platinum	79 197 **Au** Gold	80 201 **Hg** Mercury	81 204 **Tl** Thallium	82 207 **Pb** Lead	83 209 **Bi** Bismuth	84 209 **Po** Polonium	85 210 **At** Astatine	86 222 **Rn** Radon
110 271 **Ds** Darmstadtium	111 272 **Rg** Roentgenium	112 277 **Uub** Ununbium		114 289 **Uuq** Ununquadium		116 292 **Uuh** Ununhexium		

65 159 **Tb** Terbium	66 163 **Dy** Dysprosium	67 165 **Ho** Holmium	68 167 **Er** Erbium	69 169 **Tm** Thulium	70 173 **Yb** Ytterbium	71 175 **Lu** Lutetium
97 247 **Bk** Berkelium	98 251 **Cf** Californium	99 252 **Es** Einsteinium	100 257 **Fm** Fermium	101 258 **Md** Mendelevium	102 259 **No** Nobelium	103 262 **Lr** Lawrencium

caustic Capable of burning the skin or eating away other delicate items by a chemical reaction.

compost Mixture of decayed plants and other organic material used by gardeners as a fertilizer.

corrode To be changed or destroyed by a chemical reaction, as when metals rust.

density A measure of mass based on a unit of volume.

electrolysis The process of passing electricity through a substance to cause a chemical reaction, which can in certain circumstances reduce a substance into its elemental parts.

impurity A small amount of a substance that contaminates a larger amount of another substance.

leavening agent A substance used in doughs and batters that causes them to rise.

lye A strong solution of sodium hydroxide or potassium hydroxide in water that is used in industrial cleaners.

mineral oil An oil obtained from fossil fuels, such as kerosene.

neutralize To make a substance neither acidic nor alkaline.

oxidize The loss of one or more electrons by a molecule, atom, or ion.

propellant A substance that is burned to give thrust to a rocket, aircraft, or spacecraft.

radioactive Describing an element that decays over time by a process involving the nucleus, releasing potentially harmful particles in the process.

refine To produce a purer form of something by removing the impurities from it.

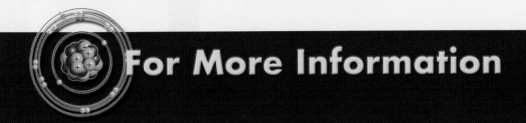

American Chemical Society
1155 Sixteenth Street NW
Washington, DC 20036
(800) 227-5558
E-mail: webmaster@acs.org
Web site: http://www.acs.org

American Chemistry Council
1300 Wilson Boulevard
Arlington, VA 22209
(703) 741-5000
Web site: http://www.americanchemistry.com

Chemical Heritage Foundation
315 Chestnut Street
Philadelphia, PA 19106
(215) 925-2222
E-mail: info@chemheritage.org
Web site: http://www.chemheritage.org

The Electrochemical Society
65 South Main Street, Building D
Pennington, NJ 08534-2839
(609) 737-1902
E-mail: ecs@electrochem.org
Web site: http://www.electrochem.org

Smithsonian Institute
P.O. Box 37012
SI Building, Room 153, MRC 010
Washington, DC 20013-7012
(202) 633-1000
E-mail: info@si.edu
Web site: http://www.si.edu

Web Sites

Due to the changing nature of Internet links, Rosen Publishing has developed an online list of Web sites related to the subject of this book. This site is updated regularly. Please use this link to access the list:

http://www.rosenlinks.com/uept/pota

For Further Reading

Blashfield, Jean F. *Potassium.* Austin, TX: Raintree Steck-Vaugn Publishers, 2001.

Churchhill, E. Richard, Louis V. Loeschnig, and Muriel Mandell. *365 Simple Science Experiments with Everyday Materials.* New York, NY: Black Dog & Levenhall Publishers, Inc., 1997.

Cobb, Vicky. *Fireworks.* Minneapolis, MN: Millbrook Press, 2006.

Pough, Frederick H. Peterson. *First Guide to Rocks and Minerals.* New York, NY: Houghton Mifflin, 1991.

Stwertka, Albert. *A Guide to the Elements.* Oxford, England: Oxford University Press, 2002.

Woodford, Chris. *Potassium.* Tarrytown, NY: Benchmark Books, 2003.

Worth, Richard. *Gunpowder.* New York, NY: Chelsea House, 2003.

Bibliography

Blashfield, Jean F. *Potassium.* Austin, TX: Raintree Steck-Vaugn Publishers, 2001.

DK Staff. *The DK Science Encyclopedia.* New York, NY: DK Publishing, 1998.

Emsley, John. *Nature's Building Blocks: An A–Z Guide to the Elements.* Oxford, England: Oxford University Press, 2001.

Fairchild, Jim. "The Searles Valley Saline Mineral Resource Historical Chemical Extraction Facilities." Searles Lake Gem & Mineral Society.

February 20, 2004. Retrieved October 10, 2006 (http://www1.iwvisp.com/tronagemclub/history1.htm).

Food and Nutrition Board. "Dietary Reference Intakes: Water, Potassium, Sodium, Chloride, and Sulfate." Institute of Medicine of the National Academies. February 4, 2004. Retrieved October 10, 2006 (http://www.iom.edu/CMS/3788/3969/18495.aspx).

Knapp, Brian. *Acids, Bases, and Salts.* Danbury, CT: Grolier Educational, 1998.

Knapp, Brian. *Sodium and Potassium.* Danbury, CT: Grolier Educational, 1996.

March, Robert H. "Atom." *World Book Multimedia Encyclopedia.* Chicago, IL: World Book Inc., 2001.

National Pesticide Telecommunications Network. "Potassium Salts of Fatty Acids." August 2001. Retrieved October 3, 2006 (http://npic.orst.edu/factsheets/psfagen.pdf#search=% 22Potassium% 20insecticide% 22).

PotashCorp. "PotashCorp Fact Sheet." Retrieved September 12, 2006 (http://www.potashcorp.com/media/pdf/about/PCS_FactSheet.pdf).

Usselman, Melvyn C. "Chemistry." *World Book Multimedia Encyclopedia.* Chicago, IL: World Book Inc., 2001.

Wikipedia.com. "Potash Corporation of Saskatchewan." July 6, 2006. Retrieved September 12, 2006 (http://en.wikipedia.org/wiki/Potash_Corporation_of_Saskatchewan).

Wikipedia.com. "Potassium permanganate." September 12, 2006. Retrieved September 13, 2006 (http://en.wikipedia.org/wiki/Potassium_permanganate).

Woodford, Chris. *Potassium.* Tarrytown, NY: Benchmark Books, 2003.

Index

A

acids, 20–22, 39
alkali metals, 16, 18–19
atomic number, 13
atomic weight, 11, 15–16
atoms, structure of, 12–13

B

bases, 20–22, 39

D

Davy, Sir Humphry, 8–9, 23

E

electrolysis, 8, 9
electrolytes, 35–36, 37
electrons, 12–13, 15, 16, 18, 20, 32, 36, 37

F

fertilizers, 9, 22, 24, 28–30, 34

G

glass, 7, 9, 26, 28
gunpowder and fireworks, 9, 26, 32–33, 34

H

halogens, 18, 19

I

ions, 16, 18, 20, 22, 23, 24, 28, 30, 35, 36, 37, 38
isotopes, 16, 33

K

Klaproth, Martin, 8

M

Mendeleyev, Dmitry, 10–11

N

neutrons, 12, 15
nucleus, 12, 13, 18, 33

P

pearlash, 25–26
periodic table, 10–11, 13–18
pH scale, 22
potash, 6–9, 23, 25, 26, 28
potassium
    history of, 6–9
    in the human body, 16, 35–39
    reactivity of, 4, 6, 13, 16, 18–19, 20, 26–27
    uses of, 4–5, 6, 9, 22, 28–34
    where it can be found, 4, 6, 8, 23–25
potassium aluminum silicate, 28
potassium-argon dating, 33

potassium carbonate, 5, 7, 25, 31, 32

potassium chloride (sylvite), 8, 9, 23,
    25, 26, 30

potassium hydroxide (caustic potash),
    7–8, 9, 20, 22, 30–31

potassium nitrate, 24–25, 26, 32

potassium superoxide, 4–5

protons, 12, 13, 15, 16, 20, 33, 37

R

reactivity series, 20

soaps and cleansers, 7, 9, 20, 22, 24,
    26, 30–31

sodium carbonate (soda ash), 8

Volta, Alessandro, 9

W

World War II, 26

About the Author

Greg Roza has written and edited educational materials for children for the past seven years. He has a master's degree in English from the State University of New York at Fredonia. Roza has long had an interest in scientific topics, including chemistry, and spends much of his spare time tinkering with machines around the house. He lives in Hamburg, New York, with his wife, Abigail, and his three children, Autumn, Lincoln, and Daisy.

Photo Credits

Cover, pp. 1, 13, 15, 17, 40–41 by Tahara Anderson; p. 7 © Jacques Jangoux/Photo Researchers, Inc.; p. 8 © Bettmann/Corbis; p. 10 © SSPL/The Image Works; p. 19 (top) © Martyn F. Chillmaid/Photo Researchers, Inc.; pp. 19 (bottom), 27 © Andrew Lambert Photography/Photo Researchers, Inc.; pp. 21, 34 Mark Golebiowski; p. 24 © Martin Land/Photo Researchers, Inc.; p. 25 © Private Collection/The Bridgeman Art Library; p. 29 © Robert Brook/Photo Researchers, Inc.; pp. 30, 32, 38 Shutterstock.com; p. 31 © Joel W. Rogers/Corbis; p. 36 © Digital Stock; p. 39 © Will & Deni Mcintyre/Photo Researchers, Inc.

Designer: Tahara Anderson; **Editor:** Nicholas Croce
Photo Researcher: Cindy Reiman